MADELINE AT THE WHITE HOUSE

THE TOMB OF T

MADELINE
AT THE WHITE HOUSE

Story and pictures by
John Bemelmans Marciano

PUFFIN BOOKS

For Galatea

PUFFIN BOOKS
An imprint of Penguin Random House LLC
375 Hudson Street
New York, New York 10014

First published in the United States of America by Viking,
an imprint of Penguin Young Readers Group, 2011
Published by Puffin Books, an imprint of Penguin Random House LLC, 2016

THE LIBRARY OF CONGRESS HAS CATALOGED THE VIKING EDITION AS FOLLOWS:
Marciano, John Bemelmans. Madeline at the White House / story and pictures by John Bemelmans Marciano.
Summary: Madeline and the other orphans of the vine-covered house in Paris spend
Easter at the White House visiting with the President's daughter.
ISBN 978-0-670-01228-2 (hardcover)
[1. Stories in Rhyme. 2. Presidents—Family—Fiction. 3. White House (Washington, D.C.)—Fiction.
4. Easter—Fiction. 5. Orphans—Fiction. 6. Washington (D.C.)—Fiction.]
I. Title. PZ8.3.M368Mb 2011
[E]—dc22 2010025110

Puffin Books ISBN 978-1-101-99780-2

Manufactured in China

1 3 5 7 9 10 8 6 4 2

In an old white house in Washington, D.C.,

Lived as lonely a girl as there can be.
Her name was Miss Penelope Randall,
But everyone always called her Candle
On account of a wildly stubborn curl
That like a flame would dance and twirl.

She needed an appointment to see her father.
But he always canceled so why did she bother?

She sat bored and alone at her desk and stool,
The only student of the White House school.

Secret Service Agent Downs

Made sure she never left the grounds.

But life took a turn for the better
When from her mother came a letter.
It read:

PAR AVION

Miss Candle Randall
1600 Pennsylvania Avenue
Washington, D.C.
U.S.A.

THE FIRST LADY

Candle, my dear,   Bombay
Sorry to miss Easter again this year.
But in my place I've arranged to send
The daughter and classmates
        of a very good friend.
Their old house in Paris
        is covered with vines
And they travel about
        in two straight lines.
                (over)

Their plane gets in at half past nine.

The smallest one is Madeline.

Eleven girls were very shy,
But Madeline looked her straight in the eye
And said to Candle, "How do you do?
It's very nice to be meeting you."

The girls were taken to their quarters.

"Time to unpack," were Miss Clavel's orders.

Madeline's bag contained a SURPRISE!

A rabbit! Or rather, a friend in disguise.

Madeline's magician had stowed away
To join them for the holiday.
The girls all cried "Hip hip HOORAY!"

And went to Candle's room to play.

The girls bid good night to their new friend.

Candle was sad that it had to end.

She went to bed without delay.

She could hardly wait for the following day.

The White House Easter celebration

Is the most fun festival in the nation!

They hunted Easter eggs at noon,

And then they rolled them with a spoon.

Ice cream, pie, and chocolate cake

Can lead to quite a tummyache.

Madeline asked, "Would it be all right
If I stayed in Candle's room tonight?"
Miss Clavel weakly nodded yes.
(Her stomach too was in distress.)
"Just go to sleep early—that's a warning!
Our plane leaves first thing in the morning."

They played dress-up,

Cards,

And had a lark,

And told scary stories in the dark.

But when the cuckoo sang the hour
The frolicking mood turned quickly sour.
The night—where could it have gone?
All too soon would come the dawn.
Madeline would soon be leaving—
Oh, how Candle started grieving!

The poor girl cried, "Boohoo!
Why can't I fly away too?
Outside my window the world looks pretty
But I've never even seen the city."

The rabbit took this as his cue—
A magician knows just what to do.
He raised his arms like a candelabra
And chanted the word "ABRACADABRA!"

The rabbit conjured something awesome:
A magic tide of cherry blossom!

Had two girls ever flown so high

Up into the starry sky?

The rising sun erased the moon.
Miss Clavel would wake up soon.

But on and on they tempted fate.

They were almost home . . .

Perhaps too late!
From the hall outside, Miss Clavel knocked
And tried the door, but it was locked.
"Are you there, Madeline? We're in a hurry!"
Said Miss Clavel, quite sick with worry.

Agent Downs, a good bit bolder,
Broke the door open with his shoulder.

The girls, they saw, were fast asleep.
But there was a schedule to keep.

Miss Clavel said, "Madeline, make haste,
We haven't any time to waste."

To say good-bye is always sad,

But coming home is never bad.

Miss Clavel came in that night

And checked the girls by candlelight.

To all the beds she walked around

To see the girls were safe and sound.

Then with a smile, she closed the door.

That's all there is, there isn't any more.

A background note to MADELINE AT THE WHITE HOUSE

The idea for sending Madeline to the White House was my grandfather's and grew out of his friendship with Jacqueline Kennedy. In a series of letters from late 1961 and early 1962, my grandfather sounded out the First Lady on ideas for the book, which he proposed calling "Madeline Visits Caroline," with text by Mrs. Kennedy herself. At the time, he was still working on "Madeline and the Magician," an expanded version of "Madeline's Christmas." In this book the Magician, named Mustapha, was sent away by Miss Clavel, but returned at the end in the form of a lonely meowing cat wearing a fez, a ruse that would allow him to stay with the girls forever.

My grandfather died in 1962, before the Magician book was finished or the White House one even begun. A proud veteran of the First World War, he was buried in Arlington Cemetery, which you will find on the endpapers of this book. Although French was his first language and he grew up largely in Germany, my grandfather immigrated to New York as a teenager and considered himself first and foremost a proud American.

One of my favorite pictures of my grandfather's is the sketch for the final page of "Madeline and the Magician," in which Mustapha the cat is surrounded by the girls. I imagine that it is actually my grandfather who is the magician, and certainly it is Madeline and the girls with whom he will stay forever.

J.B.M.

Places visited in the book:

At the White House
Oval Office
Lincoln Bedroom
South Lawn

On the Magic Ride
Lincoln Memorial
Dome of the Capitol
Jefferson Memorial
Washington Monument

On the Endpapers
Arlington National Cemetery

THE TOMB OF THE

HERE RESTS IN
HONORED GLORY
AN AMERICAN
SOLDIER
KNOWN
NKNOWN SOLDIER